SHADOW
SQUADRON

# STEEL HAMMER

STONE ARCH BOOKS
a capstone imprint

SHADOW
SQUADRON

# STEEL HAMMER

WRITTEN BY
CARL BOWEN

ILLUSTRATED BY
WILSON TORTOSA

AND
BENNY FUENTES

COVER ART BY
MARC LEE

2012.241

*AUTHORIZING*

Shadow Squadron is published by
Stone Arch Books,
A Capstone Imprint,
1710 Roe Crest Drive
North Mankato, MN 56003
www.capstonepub.com

Cataloging-in-Publication Data is available on the
Library of Congress website.

ISBN: 978-1-4965-0385-5 (library binding)
ISBN: 978-1-4965-0389-3 (paperback)

Summary: Shadow Squadron has never had an
easy mission, but under Lieutenant Commander
Ryan Cross's leadership, the team has routinely
achieved the impossible. But this time, the team
has an especially tall order: parachute onto a
moving train, secure a large cache of weapons, and
neutralize the elite ISIS soldiers on board.

Printed in China by Nordica
0415/CA21500557
042015  008839NORDF15

# CONTENTS

1316.981

2012.101

ACCESS GRANTED

# CLASSIFIED

## SHADOW SQUADRON DOSSIER

### CROSS, RYAN

RANK: Lieutenant Commander
BRANCH: Navy SEAL
PSYCH PROFILE: Cross is the team leader of Shadow Squadron. Control oriented and loyal, Cross insisted on hand-picking each member of his squad.

PHOTO NOT AVAILABLE

### PAXTON, ADAM

RANK: Sergeant First Class
BRANCH: Army (Green Beret)
PSYCH PROFILE: Paxton has a knack for filling the role most needed in any team. His loyalty makes him a born second-in-command.

### YAMASHITA, KIMIYO

RANK: Lieutenant
BRANCH: Army Ranger
PSYCH PROFILE: The team's sniper is an expert marksman and a true stoic. It seems his emotions are as steady as his trigger finger.

## LANCASTER, MORGAN

RANK: Staff Sergeant
BRANCH: Air Force Combat Control
PSYCH PROFILE: The team's newest member is a tech expert who learns fast and has the ability to adapt to any combat situation.

## JANNATI, ARAM

4236.052

PHOTO NOT AVAILABLE

RANK: Second Lieutenant
BRANCH: Army Ranger
PSYCH PROFILE: Jannati serves as the team's linguist. His sharp eyes serve him well as a spotter, and he's usually paired with Yamashita on overwatch.

## SHEPHERD, MARK

1216.062

PHOTO NOT AVAILABLE

RANK: Lieutenant
BRANCH: Army (Green Beret)
PSYCH PROFILE: The heavy-weapons expert of the group, Shepherd's love of combat borders on unhealthy.

2019.681

## MISSION BRIEFING

OPERATION

### STEEL HAMMER
### 012

Official orders have come down for us to travel to Iraq. The memo states we'll be training local forces to defend themselves from Islamic State insurgents, but that's just a cover story. Our actual assignment will be to sabotage ISIS equipment in order to interreupt their supply chain.

In short, we're going to be clogging the gears of their war machine. Stay sharp, people, or we'll get chewed up, too.

— Lieutenant Commander Ryan Cross

3245.98 ● ● ●

IRAQ

## PRIMARY OBJECTIVE(S)

- Sabotage ISIS supply chain

- Rendezvous with Peshmerga forces

1932.789

## SECONDARY OBJECTIVE(S)

- Secure any munitions found

0412.981

1624.054

## INTEL

\*DECRYPTING\*

12345

## COM CHATTER

- ISIS: the terrorist organization Islamic State of Iraq and Syria. Also referred to as the Islamic State of Iraq and Levant, or the Islamic State of Iraq and al-Sham.

- KEVLAR: bullet-resistant fabric

- PESHMERGA: military force of Iraqi Kurdistan

- NEOPRENE: flexible synthetic rubber that prevents leaking

3245.98 ● ● ●

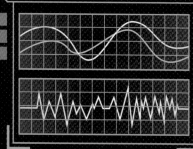

# MOVING TARGETS

Lieutenant Commander Ryan Cross had done plenty of parachuting throughout his military career. From emergency bailouts to controlled insertions deep behind enemy lines, he'd handled jumps in all conditions under all sorts of circumstances. He'd never so much as bruised a heel on a jump. The idea that he might be scared to take the long fall was completely out of the question.

With all that said, Cross definitely had his misgivings about this particular jump.

One point against it was that he was behind enemy lines — *deep* behind enemy lines. He had no direct support from his government, only the aid of friendly local forces. Secondly, it was a night jump, which was more than a little risky over unfamiliar, unfriendly territory. Modern GPS and night-vision technology alleviated most of the foreseeable complications, but the risk was still there.

Lastly, this jump was a HALO jump — high-altitude, low-opening. Cross and his team had walked out of their MC130-J Commando II on a very precise schedule at some 30,000 feet and wouldn't open their chutes until they were only 2,500 feet off the ground. That left Cross very little time to react if his main chute's lines got tangled, or if the thing simply didn't deploy, and he had to activate his reserve chute.

But none of those factors concerned Cross too much. He'd done plenty of night jumps, HALO jumps, and jumps into enemy territory. No, his main area of concern was this mission's unusual landing zone: *the top of a moving train.*

This particular train was moving south through northern Iraq, from Mosul toward Baiji, but Cross meant to stop it well before it got to that city. The train was manned by members of the Islamic State terrorist group, ISIS. Its cargo included weapons, ammunition, and desperate prisoners all taken from central Iraq when ISIS had begun expanding its influence across that region.

ISIS's prisoners were packed into two passenger cars behind the engine. The next three boxcars were stacked high with crates of stolen war goods — much of which had come from the US in the first place. The rest of the cars were either tankers full of oil or flatbeds carrying pickup trucks, jeeps, and Humvees. Five guards rode outside the train. Mission intel suggested that at least another seven were positioned throughout the interior.

Four of the five exterior guards were positioned on top of the train in teams of two. They were placed behind heavy machine guns mounted on tripods, which were surrounded by sandbag barriers. One gun stood atop the first prisoner car. The second gun stood atop the last car full of weapons. The last exterior guard sat at ease at the very rear of the train, smoking a cigarette as he dangled his feet above

the tracks. An AK-47 lay across his lap. None of the guards outside had yet noticed Cross or his team approaching. Things were about to get ugly.

Taking a slow, calming breath, Cross tapped the touchscreen of the datapad bound to the inside of his left forearm in a Kevlar and neoprene bracer. On it was an altimeter reading at the top and a circle with the words "Go Time" written in the center. The altimeter reading turned from green to yellow to red, and then the circle turned red as well. Both began to flash.

Cross tapped the screen right in the center of the circle. That sent the message to the other three soldiers falling behind him, as well as to the overwatch team waiting on a rise about 500 yards away from the landing zone. The train was still well behind them and the jumpers were still well more than 2000 feet above the ground. But according to the math, it was now or never.

"Go time," he said into the mouthpiece of his oxygen bottle. The old thrill rose within him. It heated his blood and sharpened his senses to battle readiness as he yanked the ripcord.

The team Cross led was codenamed Shadow Squadron: a covert, black-tier, special missions unit of the US armed forces. Formed by and answering to the Joint Special Operations Command of the greater US Special Operations Command, the eight-soldier team consisted of the cream of the elite of special operations soldiers from all four branches of the military. Cross was a Navy SEAL, but he commanded Green Berets, Army Rangers, a Marine from the Special Operations Regiment, an Air Force Combat Controller, and even a former CIA operative from the agency's Special Activities Division.

Together, the team took on assignments in situations or areas where the US military had an interest but couldn't be seen taking direct action. Shadow Squadron's existence was secret, its tech was top of the line, and its budget was astronomical and well camouflaged. It was no surprise that the team's mission record was nearly spotless.

Cross had lost men to death, injury, and even a better job offer, but his team always got the job done.

They'd fought pirates off the coast of Somalia, human traffickers in Mali, drug-runners in Colombia, rogue American mercenaries in the Gulf of Mexico, Russian Spetznaz in the bitter cold of Antarctica, and a whole rogues' gallery of criminals, terrorists, and other enemies of the state all around the world.

Like avenging ghosts, the squad went where it was needed, did what it was called upon to do, and disappeared.

Cross's time with Shadow Squadron was the high mark of his career, the service he was most proud of. It didn't bother him that he earned no glory in the work due to the highly secret and sensitive nature of his assignments. That wasn't why he did the job. Knowing that he had led his team with honor, courage, and professionalism was more than enough of a reward for him.

Well, that and the times he got to feed his inner adrenaline junkie by doing something like HALO-jumping behind enemy lines onto the back of a moving train in the dead of night.

* * *

With Cross in the sky were Sergeant First Class Adam Paxton, a Green Beret, and Cross's second in command; Sergeant Mark Shepherd, another Green Beret; and Second Lieutenant Aram Jannati from the Marine Special Operations Regiment.

Upon receiving the "Go Time" signal, all four men opened their chutes at once and pitched themselves downward over the railroad tracks. Cross took the sudden kick of deceleration like a boxer taking a shot in the gut. He got his descent under control ahead of them. He didn't have much time to line up, match speed, and aim for a flat part of the train. Fortunately, the train wasn't going terribly fast, so landing on it wasn't going to feel *too* much like getting hit by a speeding car.

Unfortunately, the sound of the engine and the rumble and clack of the wheels on the tracks weren't enough to mask the sound of four parachutes popping so low overhead. As Cross craned his neck to look at the train coming up below and behind them, he saw the men at the machine gun nests bolt upright and begin looking around frantically. He couldn't spare more than a moment to take note, though, as the ground was rushing up awfully fast and the train's engine compartment was just passing below him.

*No time to worry about the machine gunners,* he thought. *Focus. Focus . . .*

All at once, Cross hauled backward on his jump rigging, lurched out of his breakneck dive, and swung forward beneath his parachute like a kid on a playground. Hoping he'd judged his momentum correctly, Cross cut away the parachute right at the edge of the forward swing so that all of his momentum continued to carry him forward along with the direction of the train. He'd practiced the maneuver dozens of times in preparation for the mission, but even though he now pulled it off just as he'd practiced, he hit the train an awful lot harder than he expected.

## THUD!

The impact knocked the wind out of him. He wasted precious seconds gasping for air that wouldn't come. He got up to a knee with a wall of gray closing in around his vision, his hands numbly trying to unsling his M4 carbine from its rig. The landing had left him one boxcar away from the forward machine gun position. As his black silk parachute drifted away into the night, he saw one of the two ISIS men in their sandbag nest looking at him in stupefied awe. The other man awkwardly swung his M60E4 machine gun around to take aim.

* * *

Salvation came from 500 yards away in the darkness. From a blind on a rise overlooking the train tracks, Lieutenant Kimiyo Yamashita — an Army Ranger and the team's primary sniper — lay hidden on overwatch along with Staff Sergeant Morgan Lancaster — a USAF Combat Controller. Staring down the night-sights of the Leupold scope mounted atop his M110 sniper rifle, Yamashita squeezed off a single shot. His bullet neutralized the man at the forward machine gun as a threat.

From Cross's perspective, there was no muzzle flash and no sound of a shot. One moment the man was bringing his machine gun to bear, the next he'd slumped forward over it.

For her part, Lancaster neutralized the other three Islamic State men atop the train with a single touch on the tablet computer before her. The device was connected wirelessly to three extremely advanced weapons systems called autoguns. They were set up around the overwatch position, each with an M110 sniper rifle settled into a nest of servos and actuators. They could move them smoothly and quickly across a range of 45 degrees up, down, left, or right from their starting positions.

Atop each rifle was a $10,000 three-lens rifle scope that included state-of-the-art range-finding and tracking hardware and a high-definition infrared camera. All of it was connected back to Lancaster's tablet. With the device, she could mark a target in each scope's field of vision, set the autoguns to track said targets, and command them to fire with a simple tap on the screen.

As she made that tap now, the other three ISIS soldiers at the two machine gun sites fell dead at their posts. It had been only seconds after they'd realized that five armed men were parachuting onto the top of their train.

"Got my three," Lancaster said to Yamashita with a self-satisfied grin. They watched as one of the two men she'd shot off the rear machine gun nest slumped over and rolled off the side of the train. "How you doing, John Henry?"

Lancaster's playful tone annoyed Yamashita, but he kept his eyes glued to his Leupold scope, watching the Islamic State man at the rear of the train. That man hadn't noticed the four Shadow Squadron soldiers landing atop the cars, but he certainly did notice when the body of one of his comrades bounced past him on the ground and rolled away from the train. Grabbing up his rifle in a panic, the man stood and began to make his way across the last flatbed toward the front of the train to investigate. Sighting down on him, Yamashita pulled the trigger.

## POP!

"Don't brag," he said softly as the last guard fell dead, leaving a gruesome smear across the back bumper of the stolen Humvee lashed to the flatbed in front of him. "Your computer's doing the hard part for you."

Lancaster let out a low, impressed whistle through her teeth. "Show-off," she whispered.

Yamashita gave her a nod and tapped the two-way canalphone nestled in his left ear.

* * *

"Clear," overwatch reported.

Cross tapped his canalphone as he climbed to his feet, finally able to take a breath. "Roger that," he said, sucking wind. "Police your gear and rendezvous with Clean-Up."

"Sir," Yamashita's voice replied in his ear. "Out."

Cross surveyed the top of the train through the lens of his AN/PSQ-20 night-vision system while unslinging his M4 and sliding a round into the chamber. Farther back he could see Paxton double-checking the two dead men at the second machine gun nest. Shepherd was climbing up on the back of the rear weapons car. Jannati was moving forward across the top of the nearest oil tanker car.

"Fireteam, we're clear," Cross said, relaying overwatch's report to the other three men. "Status report?"

"Fine, sir," Paxton said.

"I'm all right," Shepherd said. He sounded as jacked up on adrenaline as Cross felt. "Nearly missed the train, but I got a toe on it at the last second. Holy cow, man. Whose idea was this, anyway?"

*Yours, you ham,* Cross thought with a wry grin.

"My cutaway got stuck for a second," Jannati reported from the rear of the train. "I missed by a couple of cars, but I'm coming up now."

"Eyes open," Cross said. "No way they missed us thumping down on top of this thing. When they don't hear from their friends, they're going to send somebody up to investigate."

As if on cue, a cell phone next to the dead machine gunner lit up and started buzzing.

"Gather up," Cross said. "And get ready."

"Sir," the men responded.

Moments later, the other three soldiers joined up with Cross. Fortunately, no one from inside the train had emerged to investigate the noise they made coming together.

However, both dead machine gunners' cell phones started ringing.

"Listen up, here's the play," Cross said quickly and quietly. "I'm going forward to secure the engine. I want you —" he pointed at Shepherd "—to come down the back of this car and get ready by the door."

Shepherd nodded.

Cross looked at Paxton and Jannati, "I want you two on the second car, one on each end. On my signal, we all go in together, neutralize the IS targets, and secure the prisoners. When that's done, I'll come back and stop the train. After that, we'll sweep and clear the boxcars. When there's nobody left, we'll call for Clean-Up. Everybody got it?"

His men nodded.

"Let's do it."

## INTEL

*DECRYPTING*

12345

## COM CHATTER

- AL-QAEDA: a global terrorist organization
- CALIPH: a political and religious leader believed to be the successor to Mohammed, the Koran's prophet
- IED: Improvised Explosive Device, which is a handmade bomb

3245.98

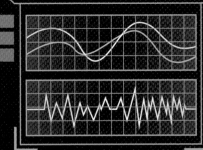

# OIL AND RELIGION

The assignment that had given rise to Shadow Squadron's current mission in Iraq had come to them some weeks ago. Back home at the team's stateside headquarters and command center, Cross came into his mission briefing room with Paxton, his second, at his side. The other six members of the team were already there and waiting around the conference table. Paxton headed for his seat by the head of the table, dragging a finger across the tablet computer screen recessed into the table's surface. The touchscreen blinked to life, as did the computer whiteboard on the wall at the far end of the room. Both screens displayed the sword-and-globe emblem of Joint Special Operations Command.

"Morning," Cross said, moving to the head of the room to stand before the whiteboard. "Some of you have heard the rumors already, but let me be the first to confirm them for you. Orders have come down for a long-term deployment. We're going to Iraq as part of the 300."

From the opposite end of the table, Shepherd was the first to react. He sat up straight with a big grin and immediately began quoting lines from a similarly named movie he loved.

"This is where we fight," he growled in a cartoonish imitation of the main character's accent.

"This is where they die!" Jannati chimed in. He was almost as big a fan of the movie as Shepherd.

"Give them nothing," Shepherd said, nodding at Jannati.

"But take from them everything!" Jannati said.

Paxton glanced their way. "Guys, settle down," he said. Paxton didn't raise his voice or so much as frown at them. He simply let the gravity of his tone do all the work.

"Sorry," Jannati said, still grinning.

Around the table, the others' reactions were mixed. Lancaster simply nodded, accepting the news. Williams wrinkled his nose like he'd smelled something bad. Carter Howard — the team's newest member, on permanent loan from the CIA's Special Activities Division — rolled his eyes, shook his head, and smirked.

The most telling and subtle reaction came from Yamashita. For a moment, the sniper's eyes focused inward, and he clenched his jaw so hard that the muscles around it stood out in hard white knobs. His lip twitched in what might have grown into a snarl. His eyebrows drew together for just a fraction of a second. The whole expression came and went in a blink before the sniper's usual calm, professional façade returned — but not before Cross saw it play out on the stoic soldier's face.

Cross could hardly fault Yamashita for the anger and distaste. To dramatically understate the case, the United States had a complicated relationship with the nation of Iraq. From the 1960s to the 1990s,

foreign affairs between the two had swung back and forth from the US arming Kurdish rebels in their fight against Iraq's dictatorial anti-Western government to supplying Iraq with chemical weapons to use against their neighbor Iran. In the early '90s, the US even took up arms against Iraq directly when Iraq tried to annex and conquer its southern neighbor Kuwait in an attempt to seize Kuwait's oil wealth in order to pay off Iraq's vast war debts.

The short war that ensued resulted in Iraq's inferior armed forces being pushed back out of Kuwait, as well as a cease-fire agreement that called for the destruction of Iraq's chemical weapons arsenal, regular inspections by the United Nations, and a no-fly zone enforced by US air power.

Iraq's tyrannical leader, Saddam Hussein, remained in power, however. The US allowed him to do pretty much whatever he wanted within Iraq itself. While the CIA covertly funded, armed, and trained dissident groups within Iraq, the US did nothing when Hussein brutally cracked down and killed his own people to maintain his power. The prevailing attitude from the United States seemed to be that it wanted Saddam Hussein removed from power, but it would rather the Iraqis did the job themselves. The most the US did from the end of the war to the end of the century was repeatedly warn Iraq about its failure to comply with the terms of the war's cease-fire agreement.

Relations between Iraq and the US steadily worsened. Unable to deny or ignore the way Saddam Hussein ruled Iraq, American President George W. Bush decided that the time had come to remove Hussein from power. He tried to make the argument that removing Hussein made America itself safer because then Iraq wouldn't be able to use its hidden stockpile of chemical weapons or supply them to terrorists who could use them against America itself (this despite the fact that there was no conclusive evidence that Iraq had such weapons any longer).

When diplomacy finally broke down for good, the US led a coalition of allied nations against the armies of Iraq. As before, the vastly superior coalition forces quickly prevailed, toppling the Iraqi regime and capturing Iraq's capital.

In a perfect world, that would have been the

end of the matter. But rather than surrendering, forces loyal to the Iraqi regime splintered and hid throughout the nation, leading guerilla attacks against the occupying forces.

Making matters worse, certain terrorist groups — Al-Qaeda not the least among them — sent weaponry and soldiers into Iraq to aid the deposed insurgents. Its government in ruins, Iraq plunged into a state of civil war.

For the next eight years, American combat forces remained in Iraq. Their supposed mission was to help maintain the peace, see to the safe installation of a new and democratically elected Iraqi government, and train the new Iraqi army to defend itself against the lingering insurgency. That latter goal, however, largely failed thanks to the ferocity and bloody-minded determination of the insurgents.

As the US commitment in Iraq dragged on, support for it faded away back home. President Bush left office, and his successor, President Barack Obama, campaigned on the promise of ending the conflict there and bringing all the troops home at long last.

For all of the previous three Presidents' high-minded talk of the need to end Saddam Hussein's tyranny and free the people of Iraq, the American people's patience was at an end. They wanted their sons and daughters and husbands and wives back home and out of harm's way once and for all. The final withdrawal of American forces from Iraq finally came at the dawn of the 21st century's second decade. It was a welcome relief to those waiting ever so anxiously for loved ones to return home.

Cross himself had spent much of his time with the SEALs in Iraq helping to root out insurgents. Most of the members of his new team had done so as well in their various capacities with their own branches of the military.

Howard had actually been there before the fighting started, helping the SAD lay the groundwork for the invasion. They knew firsthand the drudgery and monotony of fighting an invisible guerilla army for the sake of people who viewed them as interlopers and occupiers. They had seen the worst sorts of people thriving in the postwar chaos, exploiting their own people's fear and weakness and greed and religious intolerance for their own ends. Although Cross and the others had never grown tired of doing their duty, neither had they been unwilling to see that duty come to an end.

Only it wasn't really over. Now, with combat operations and the full withdrawal in the past, US troops were returning once again to Iraq. They were intended to act only as advisors and trainers for the local forces, and there were only to be some 300 or so of them. Nevertheless, the deployment was yet one more sign that America's long and complicated relationship with Iraq was far from resolved or finished.

"Begging your pardon, Commander," Shepherd said before Cross could continue, "but advising and training isn't really our strong suit."

"True," Cross said, though it technically wasn't true. Aiding and training foreign local forces was one of the core competencies of a modern special operations soldier. What Shepherd meant was that although Shadow Squadron could ably fill that role, that wasn't the sort of assignment Command generally gave them. "The truth is, we're not going to teach the locals how to do their jobs. We're going to help them swat down some noisy troublemakers once and for all. It's outside the letter of what the President says we 300 are going for, but he's not naïve. He knows this is something that needs to get done, so he wants it done right."

He paused, watching the others around the table nod — all except Yamashita. He stared blankly at the table, quietly absorbing the information like a machine.

"The problem," Cross continued, "is the terrorist group calling itself Islamic State, formerly the Islamic State of Iraq and al-Sham (Levant), or ISIS."

Cross tapped the tactical datapad strapped to his forearm and swiped a file to the touchscreen on the tabletop. A second tap brought up a recent photo on the computer whiteboard. The team saw a man in the black robes, beard, and hat of a Muslim priest. He was standing in front of an oscillating fan on the balcony of a mosque in Iraq. A pair of microphones stood before him as he gave a speech to the cameras below.

"Islamic State is led by this man," Cross went on. "Abu Bakr al-Baghdadi. He has a list of terrorist activities going back to before the invasion in 2003. We actually had him in custody for a while in 2004, but he was released and went right back to doing what he was good at. By 2010, he was the leader of Al-Qaeda in Iraq, responsible for car bombings, kidnappings, suicide bombings, IEDs — you name it. A few years later, he tried to expand his organization into Syria to profit on the civil war going on there. Without actually asking anybody, he tried to claim that Al-Qaeda in Iraq was going to be incorporating another terrorist group, Al-Nusra Front, into one organization under his leadership."

"Rude," Williams said. "Even for a terrorist."

Cross nodded. "Al-Nusra publicly rejected him for it. In fact, his methods and theology were so extreme that *Al-Qaeda* kicked him out. Not that it did much good. He'd built up enough followers by then to form his own splinter group: ISIS. Al-Baghdadi's stated goal is to establish a caliphate — an Islamic theocracy — across Syria and Iraq. Of course, he would be the head, as caliph. His group has dug its roots in deep in Syria, pushing Al-Nusra out of most of Syria and keeping President Assad's government forces out as well."

"Isn't that what we wanted?" Jannati asked. "I thought our government wanted Assad out. Weren't we on Al-Nusra's side?"

"We were on the side of the Free Syrian Army," Paxton said. "That was before Al-Nusra infiltrated it and took it over in the name of Al-Qaeda. But even though ISIS was separate from Al-Nusra, that doesn't make it better. It's a militant, extremist Sunni cult. When it moves into an area, it kills non-Sunnis, publicly rounds up anyone who raises objections, then establishes harsh Sharia laws."

"Wait," Jannati said, a look of bitter realization dawning on his face. "Were these guys connected to our White Needle situation when we were deployed in Syria?"

Not long ago, Shadow Squadron had been in Syria trying to capture two terrorists who were fleeing justice in Afghanistan and Iraq. The pair had planned to launch a stolen chemical warhead into a civilian population. The part of the whole scenario that had baffled and infuriated Jannati at the time was that the town in the warhead's sights was controlled by rebels already. Prisoners captured after the attack was foiled had claimed that the group wanted to blame Syrian President Assad for the attack in hopes of motivating the US military to step in and help them. Of course, this was before it became common knowledge that President Assad had already been using banned chemical weapons to suppress the rebellion all along.

"We think so," Cross said. "Looking back over the evidence, our analysts have come to believe that the attack was actually planned by ISIS agents to punish Al-Nusra for defying Al-Baghdadi."

Yamashita let out a sharp sigh of disgust and scowled at the table. A few of the others glanced at him, but no one said anything.

"In any case," Cross said, "Islamic State is a bigger threat now than it's ever been. It captured and now controls half the border between Iraq and Syria. A swath of northern Syria is theirs, and they're determined to march on Baghdad. Working with Sunnis across the nation, they've already seized Fallujah, Tikrit and Mosul. They're practically running the regular Iraqi army out of town without a fight. They're extremely well organized, and their early victories have allowed them to seize a treasure-trove of weapons and vehicles."

"Weapons and vehicles we left for the Iraqis," Yamashita said softly.

Cross nodded. "Taking Mosul also gave them access to the city's banks, from which the group stole more than $400 million in cash. It was well funded before, but now they have real spending power. ISIS is all over various social media sites, putting out propaganda and recruiting newcomers from all over the world. It's got the guns to put in their hands when they show up and more than enough money to feed and take care of them. From its perspective, Islamic State has nothing to worry about — its caliphate is right around the corner."

Cross paused and took a breath. "It's our job to make sure they understand just how wrong they are. Everybody got that?"

"Hoorah!" the others around the table replied — except Yamashita. He remained silently staring at the tabletop.

"Hoorah," Cross said back. "Now get your gear. We're on a plane in two hours. You're dismissed."

The team stood, excited chatter bubbling up around the table. As the others filed out, Yamashita drifted along with them, not saying anything. Cross frowned, watching him from where he stood at the head of the table. Just before the sniper left the briefing room, Cross made a decision.

"Kim," Cross said, "hang back a second."

Yamashita waited until everyone else was gone, then shut the door. He came back to his seat and stood behind it with no expression on his face.

"Commander?" he asked.

"You've got a problem with this new assignment," Cross said.

"No, sir."

"That wasn't a question, Lieutenant. The others don't read you that well, but I do. You had a real problem with our last mission in Iraq. I know you haven't forgotten our chat about it."

Yamashita clenched his jaw again and broke eye contact. It took him a moment to reply. "I did have a problem, but I got it squared away. I assumed you and I had an understanding about it."

"We do," Cross said, softening a little. "But that doesn't mean you're automatically fine. You tensed up as soon as the word Iraq came out of my mouth. Talk to me."

Yamashita took a deep breath that did little to calm him. The sniper gripped the back of his chair in white-knuckled fingers and snorted like a bull working himself up to charge.

"What is it about that place?" he said evenly. "About all those places? Why do we care so much about these deserts full of oil and religion? We keep putting weapons in the wrong people's hands, expecting them to make their lives better somehow, but they only end up hating us. It never changes. It just goes around and around forever. Are we supposed to accept that? Does Command really expect us to keep putting our lives on the line just because nobody can figure out how to get us off the treadmill of history?"

"I don't have the answers you want," Cross said, "though I wish I did. I don't know why we keep repeating our old mistakes. Maybe it's human nature."

Yamashita closed his eyes in defeat. Clearly he'd been hoping to hear something wiser or more definitive than what Cross offered.

"But there's something I do know," Cross pushed on. "People like you and me, we can't indulge ourselves with the high-minded ideals of the big picture. At our level, we don't have that luxury."

The sniper frowned, looking down at the desk once more.

"We can't obsess over what's out of our control," Cross continued. "Our job's too hard without that kind of distraction looming over us. We have to focus on the assignments in front of us. *Getting the job done, keeping each other safe.* It's up to us to play our parts and play them right. It's up to Command and the politicians to make sure those parts add up to something better than what we started with."

"But is that enough for you, Commander?" Yamashita asked. "Is that faith enough for you to keep risking your life out there?"

"That isn't why I'm willing to risk my life in the field, Lieutenant," Cross said.

Yamashita tilted his head. "So why do you?" he asked.

"Think about it," Cross said with a nod. "I'm pretty sure you already know the answer. When you figure it out, it'll answer your questions a lot better than I can."

"Let's hope so, Commander," the sniper said.

## INTEL

*DECRYPTING*

12345

## COM CHATTER

- HUMVEE: military vehicle that combines the features of a jeep with a light truck.

- M84 GRENADE: stun grenade

- MANIFEST: list of things or people aboard a given ship

- PESHMERGA: Kurdish forces of Iraqi Kurdistan

3245.98 ● ● ●

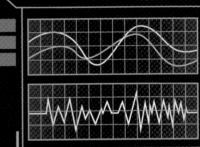

# LOCAL FORCES

*On the train . . .*

Securing and stopping the train took ten tense minutes of work. Cross and his men moved quickly and with grim determination through the engine compartment and passenger cars. They caught the Islamic State militants by surprise and took them down before they had a chance to raise an alarm. The sound and flash suppressors on the team's M4 carbines kept the people in one car from knowing what was happening in the others.

Cross, Paxton, Shepherd, and Jannati entered the passenger cars, identified the enemy militants, and eliminated them fast enough to negate any risk to their prisoners.

However, the second goal — actually stopping the train — proved more diffcult than Cross was expecting. He connected the feed from his helmet camera to Lancaster's tablet, which enabled her to see what he was seeing. In short order, she was able to walk Cross through the necessary steps to shut the engine down.

That left only the last few guards remaining. They were hidden away in the boxcars, watching over the Islamic State's shipment of stolen weapons and other equipment.

Two of the guards left their posts when the train stopped, coming forward to see what the problem was. They walked right into Jannati and Shepherd's field of fire. The last guard saw what happened to his comrades and tried to barricade himself inside the boxcar. Luckily, Paxton managed to get an M84 stun grenade through the sliding door just before the guard slammed it shut.

# FOOOOM!

The flashbang went off right at the militant's feet, disorienting him just long enough for the fire team to move up on him and surround him. Taking him prisoner would have been ideal, but when they burst in on him, they found him sitting on the floor at the rear of the boxcar with an open and overturned box of frag grenades on his lap. Bleeding from his nose and staring blindly in the direction he felt his enemies were coming from, he snatched up one of the grenades and rushed to yank off the safety clip.

## BANG!
## BANG!
## BANG!
## BANG!

Four shots rang out as one. The man lay still. The grenade rolled out of his limp fingers, the pin still firmly in place.

"Clear," Cross said.

Shepherd confirmed that the other boxcar was clear, too. No guards remained. The train was theirs.

"Call Clean-Up," Cross said.

"Sir," Paxton said.

"Inventory," Cross said to Shepherd as the four of them climbed back out of the train. "Look for a manifest. If not, just give me your best guess."

"Sir," Shepherd said.

"With me," Cross said to Jannati, leading him toward the passenger cars. Together, the two of them dragged the dead men out of the cars and moved them away from the tracks. Then they gathered the dazed, abused, and shell-shocked prisoners together under the stars. Jannati began trying to explain that they'd been rescued and that everything was going to be all right. Most of them simply stared at him without a word, either due to shock or mistrust.

The bravest of them turned out to be a French Iraqi woman in her early thirties who stepped forward as their representative. She explained that she'd been working with a team of investigators from Human Rights Watch. They'd been trying to document and expose the cruel abuses perpetrated by ISIS as its campaign of terror and conquest spread across Iraq. Many of the prisoners, like her, had been rounded up for speaking out against what ISIS was doing. Others were Shiites or Christians who'd been arrested for not being Sunnis but had promised to convert in order to save their lives. Still others had been branded criminals for breaking the strict tenets of sharia law that Islamic State had put into place. Some had no idea why they'd been rounded up. All of them had been detained in secret facilities in their hometowns where Islamic State was now in command, until that very morning when they'd all been loaded onto this train. Many assumed they were being transferred to an Islamic State prison in Baiji.

More likely, as the Human Rights Watch investigator quietly told Cross, they were being taken to an isolated location where they were going to be executed and their bodies hidden away in a mass grave. It wouldn't have been the first time that ISIS had rid itself of dissidents in such a way. She'd investigated and reported on two such sites herself — one in Syria, one in Iraq — before her capture. Knowing what she knew, it was nothing short of a miracle to her that she was still alive. That Cross and his soldiers had come when they did to free them was, she said, a miracle heaped on top of another miracle.

"Still working on that last part," Cross told her. "You think you can keep these people calm and focused and get them to come with us without a lot of fuss?"

"Maybe," she said. "Where will you take us?"

"Erbil," Cross told her.

She nodded, satisfied with the answer. Erbil lay in Iraqi Kurdistan, some 30 miles north and east of their current location. It was the largest city in that region and had thus far kept ISIS out while allowing refugees from the Islamic State's brutality to find safety within.

"I can do this," she said. "My name is Miriam, by the way."

"A pleasure to meet you, Ma'am," Cross said. "Now get them ready. We're leaving as soon as Clean-Up gets here."

Clean-Up referred to the unit consisting of the rest of Cross's team, as well as local Peshmerga forces helping out with the operation. The Peshmerga, literally translated as "those who confront death," were the local military of Iraqi Kurdistan. Less formally, the term also applied to any Kurd willing to take up arms to fight for Kurdish rights in Iraq.

The Peshmerga were no strangers to working with American military forces. They'd aided US troops throughout the invasion and subsequent insurgency. Their assistance had proven instrumental in the capture of Saddam Hussein. They'd even had a hand in capturing a crucial Al-Qaeda figure, which had contributed to the successful hunt for Osama bin Laden.

These days, with much of the regular Iraqi army in a shambles after a series of quick and demoralizing defeats by ISIS, it was the Peshmerga who were best able to stand up to the Islamic State and protect their citizens from its advances and abuses. Sunni, Shiite, Christian, Assyrian, Turkmen — they did what they could to protect them all, and they did it well. In fact, it was information from the Peshmerga that had enabled Cross's team to locate and intercept this train. And it would be the Peshmerga whom Cross counted on to protect these would-be prisoners from the Islamic State, assuming he could get everyone safely into Erbil.

The wait for Clean-Up was longer than Cross anticipated. Meanwhile, Shepherd finished his inventory. Cross and Miriam explained to the prisoners where they were headed and did what they could to answer questions, except when the questions had to do with Shadow Squadron itself.

Jannati kept a lookout. Paxton gathered up all the Islamic State militants' cell phones and took them into the train's engine compartment. He stayed by the radio and monitored the cells in an attempt to intercept any useful communications.

The Peshmerga soldiers and the rest of Cross's team showed up in three Russian-made military vehicles. Two of them were desert-camo Ural 5323 trucks. The third was a flat tan GAZ-66. The Urals were 8x8 troop transports with canvas shells over the backs. The GAZ was a smaller 4x4 with an open back that was full of soldiers. Most of them were locals, though Carter Howard sat back there with them, making them laugh. He'd worked with many of the men before and during the war, and he'd been Shadow Squadron's point of contact with them when the team had arrived.

Williams, the medic, was in the passenger seat. Yamashita and Lancaster emerged together from the back of one of the Urals. With everyone present, Shadow Squadron, the leaders of the Peshmerga platoon, Miriam, and a few inquisitive prisoners collected around Cross. Only Paxton stayed out of the huddle.

"The boxcars aren't full, but it's a good haul," Shepherd said, handing Cross a clipboard he'd found on the train. "It's mostly crates of assault rifles and ammunition, plus some lighter anti-armor and anti-personnel weapons."

Cross handed the clipboard to the leader of the Peshmerga, a lieutenant with a bald head and the lower half of one ear missing. The lieutenant frowned at it then looked at the prisoners and frowned at them too.

"Too much here for one trip," he said.

"We can get all the civilians in one Ural," Cross said. "Load up as much off the train as you can in the other one and the GAZ. We'll get the Humvees off the train, and my team will take those. We'll all make for Erbil and decide —"

"My men will take the Humvees," the Peshmerga lieutenant cut in. "They, the GAZ, and the cargo are going east into Kirkuk. We have brothers in arms there still fighting to push Islamic State out. They need what we have here more than those in Erbil."

"Qasem, this isn't what we agreed on," Howard said, trying to keep his voice friendly and reasonable. "You said —"

"We'll leave you the second Ural to take these here to safety," the lieutenant said to Cross, ignoring Howard. "We'll be back for it in the morning."

"Is this why you agreed to help us?" Cross asked, his voice low and even despite what he was thinking. "You just wanted the weapons? You knew there were civilians involved."

"I didn't know there were so many," the lieutenant said, looking down at the clipboard. Whether he meant prisoners or weapons, Cross couldn't tell. "Anyway, these are our vehicles. I decide how they are used."

"Those Humvees are US military equipment," Jannati said, scowling.

"True," the lieutenant said. "But there are many more of us here than there are of you, young man. And none of you are supposed to be here in the first place."

Howard flinched as if he'd been slapped. "Qasem! Are you seriously going to —"

"Sir?" Paxton cut in, joining the group in a hurry with a worried look on his face. "Problem." A tense silence fell over the others.

"What is it?" Cross asked, continuing to glare at the Peshmerga lieutenant.

"Communications from Mosul and Baiji have cut off," Paxton explained. "They stopped asking for the engineer over the radio. A whole bunch of calls and texts went out to the militants' phones from the same three numbers, asking what was going on and why nobody was answering. Then all the calls stopped, and nobody's tried again for five minutes. They know something's wrong."

"They will likely be here soon," Qasem said, a satisfied smile on his face. "Will you accept the loan of my truck, or would you and yours like to walk these people to Erbil?"

"We'll take it," Cross said through clenched teeth. "But don't think this will be forgotten."

"Was that an implied threat, Commander?" Qasem asked. "I think you would remember that this is not America's war anymore."

With that, Qasem walked away, drawing the rest of his men with him. He began giving orders, but his people had already started moving the weapons and other gear from the train to the Ural closest to it. Others leaped up onto the flatbeds and began untethering the stolen Humvees.

"What just happened?" Paxton asked.

"We got mugged," Jannati muttered.

"I got that guy's son out of Gitmo," Howard said, staring after Qasem in disbelief.

"All right, lock it down," Cross said. "We've got somewhere to be." He turned to Miriam. "Start getting your people in the back of that truck." He looked at Jannati and Williams. "Help her out."

The three of them moved off.

"Sir, were we counting on them to plot a safe route back to Erbil?" Lancaster asked.

Cross nodded. "Now it's your job. You'll ride up front with me. The rest of you will be in the rear with the civilians. Gather up all our gear off the other vehicles and let's move out. We're leaving in five."

Lancaster, Howard, Yamashita, and Shepherd moved off, leaving Paxton and Cross alone.

"We're not that far from Mosul," Paxton pointed out. "Baiji either. Islamic State's got to know something's wrong by now. They'll send people out to find out why nobody on the train's answering them. They probably have already."

"Probably," Cross agreed.

"Is five minutes enough to get ahead of them?"

"I hope so."

## INTEL

*DECRYPTING*

12345

## COM CHATTER

- MH-60: highly versatile version of the Sikorsky Black Hawk helicopter
- WILD BOAR: nickname for a Polish-made, all-terrain vehicle used by infantry
- URAL: Russian-made military vehicle that is similar to a Humvee

3245.98 ● ● ●

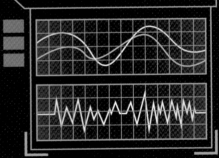

# CHAPTER FOUR

# STRIKING FIRE

The Peshmerga were still loading their vehicles when Cross's people pulled away in their truck. Ten seconds later, the sound of a helicopter came rushing in from the darkness.

## WHIR-WHIR-WHIR-WHIR

The aircraft, a Sikorsky MH-60 Black Hawk, thundered into view overhead. It shined a halogen searchlight out one of the side doors. The beam washed over Shadow Squadron's vehicle and passed to the Peshmerga working like ants. The helicopter wobbled, turned awkwardly in the air and pointed its nose down at the train.

# SHOOOM!

A second later, a missile lanced out and tore through the top of the second passenger car. The explosion split open the train and obliterated half of the Peshmerga soldiers instantly. The others scrambled for cover and started firing back.

"That's not one of ours," Lancaster whispered, half in shock. She looked back and forth between the tactical datapad on her wrist and the rearview mirror out her window.

"The Iraqis lost one of our Black Hawks when ISIS took Mosul," Cross said through gritted teeth. He was struggling to keep the overloaded 8x8 truck under some semblance of control. "We didn't figure they had anybody who could fly it."

Fortunately, whoever that pilot was, he wasn't terribly good. The helicopter's movements in the air were anything but graceful, and he'd positioned the aircraft much closer to the attack zone than he should have. As the Peshmerga began to return fire on him, the pilot had to maneuver the Black Hawk around in a huge, ungainly half-circle.

Once it was righted again, the chopper brought its M134 miniguns into firing position. And the helicopter wasn't the only Islamic State vehicle coming to fight.

"Sir, there are three Wild Boars coming up the tracks from the south," Shepherd reported in Cross's canalphone from the rear of the truck. Each one could hold 13 people and had a powerful machine gun on top. "They have ISIS flags painted on the hoods."

"Are they on our trail?" Cross asked.

Another missile streaked down from the Black Hawk, obliterating the Kurds's vehicles. The grim whine of its miniguns soon followed.

"No, sir," Shepherd said. "They're circling what's left of the train."

"We could let Qasem deal with them," Howard suggested with cold satisfaction in his voice. "He's got plenty of weapons to keep them busy with."

"Not with that Black Hawk overhead," Lancaster murmured.

Cross ground his teeth but nodded. Even caught

by surprise, the Peshmerga were plenty tough enough to deal with either the Black Hawk or three trucks worth of Islamic State soldiers. Either, but not both.

"Yamashita," Cross said. "How far's the Black Hawk from us?"

"About 900 yards," the sniper replied.

"Too far?"

"No, sir," Yamashita replied with obvious reluctance in his voice. "But we'll need to stop."

"You've got 30 seconds. One shot."

Cross ground the truck to a halt with the engine running and silently counted the seconds. At the rear, Yamashita jumped out and dropped to one knee by the side of the road. He waited for the Black Hawk to stop and hover, then he pulled the trigger.

## BANG!

Cross counted a full ten seconds after the shot, but nothing happened. The helicopter moved again and continued firing.

"No hit," Yamashita said calmly. "One more."

"Your time's up," Cross said.

"I could set up an autogun," Lancaster suggested. "It'll get the job done."

"Before I let your steam drill beat me down," Yamashita said, "I'm gonna die with a hammer in my hand."

"What?" Cross asked.

Rather than answer, Yamashita took another shot.

# BANG!

"Hey, I said one shot, Lieu —"

"Wait for it," Yamashita interrupted.

As soon as the words were out of his mouth, the Black Hawk suddenly bucked in the air, and all fire from it ceased. It pitched hard to the left and began to corkscrew down out of the sky. It hit the ground, tumbled, and caught fire as it rolled. Cross saw the whole thing in the truck's side mirror.

"I'm back in," Yamashita reported.

"Lord, lord," Lancaster said with a wry smile.

"The Black Hawk's toast," Shepherd reported from the back of the truck. "But two of the Boars are breaking off and coming this way. I guess the third one's staying to deal with the remaining Kurds."

"Good luck to them," Cross said. He slammed the truck back into gear and floored the accelerator.

The 10-ton, eight-wheel vehicle didn't exactly fly away. It more lurched off and slowly chugged up to its top speed of 50 miles per hour. For the moment, Cross had to keep it on the road while Lancaster pored over satellite maps of the area in search of a path out of harm's way — assuming one even existed. Erbil was close, but not knowing the area and driving a much slower vehicle put Cross's people at a severe disadvantage. The Wild Boars were half as heavy and had a top speed that doubled the Ural's. They were going to catch up in no time.

"Can you get us air support?" Cross asked.

"I'm trying," Lancaster said. "We don't have the air presence we used to during the war. The only inbound option is prioritizing the Peshmerga . . ."

"Figures," Cross grumbled. "How about if —"

"Sir," Paxton cut in over the canalphone, "they're going to be right on us in about a minute. Can we get off this road?"

Cross didn't even need to pass the question to Lancaster. He could see that the broken, hilly terrain would only slow the Ural down without offering any hiding places. The Boars would just catch up sooner.

"Negative," Cross said. "You're going to have to brush them back as best you can."

There came a long pause before Paxton finally replied. His voice was calm and cold, tinged with resignation. "Roger that, Commander. Out."

## INTEL

*DECRYPTING*
IIIIIIIIIIII   IIIIIIIIIIIIIIIIIIIII

## 12345

### COM CHATTER

- LEUPOLD: brand of telescopic site used for sniper rifles
- M240L: lightweight machine gun with a high rate of fire
- M67: fragmentation grenade with a 16-foot explosive radius
- PK: high-powered, Soviet-made machine gun

3245.98 ● ● ●

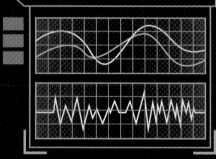

# CHAPTER FIVE

# BROTHERS-
# IN-ARMS

"You heard the man," Paxton said to the rest of the Shadow Squadron.

"What did he say?" Miriam asked from her seat near where Paxton stood.

"Things are about to get real loud, sweetheart," Shepherd said with a slightly maniacal grin.

"I want everybody up near the cab," Paxton said to the wide-eyed civilians. "Get as close to the front of the truck as you can, pack in as tight as you can, and get down. *Move!*"

The Iraqis didn't react at first, but the last word barked at them authoritatively sent them scrambling into motion. They huddled together near the front of the cargo compartment, kneeling and wrapping their arms around one another.

As they huddled, Paxton addressed his fellow soldiers. "Mark, I need you at the rear with me. Get your 240 out."

"Yeah," was all Shepherd said. He reached for his M240L machine gun where it lay packed with the rest of his gear and exchanged his M4 for it. His eyes were wild with anticipation.

"Kim, Aram, Kyle, Carter," Paxton went on, "I want a wall between us and the civilians."

"You got it," the medic said.

"Hoo, boy . . ." Howard said.

Yamashita just nodded.

"Wait," Jannati said. "Let me get back there with you guys. I can do more good shooting than —"

Paxton didn't shake his head or raise his voice. He simply laid a hand on Jannati's shoulder and said softly, "We'll handle it, Marine."

"They're coming up in range," Shepherd said. He knelt by the truck's tailgate and propped his machine gun on it. "You ready?"

Jannati nodded at Paxton and backed off. Paxton turned to the rear of the truck and knelt beside Shepherd. Jannati, Williams, Howard, and Yamashita moved to the edge of where the Iraqis huddled. They turned around and positioned as much of themselves as they could between the unarmed civilians and what was about to come.

Paxton looked at Shepherd and gave him a nod as the two Wild Boars charged forward, cutting off a bend in the road to catch up. When they regained the road, Islamic State soldiers came up out of the armored roof of each vehicle and took up the PK machine guns on top.

"*De oppresso liber*," Paxton said solemnly.

Shepherd snorted out half a laugh and rolled his eyes. "*Semper ubi, sub ubi*," he replied.

Then a storm of bullets filled the air.

# BOOM BANG BOOM BANG BOOM

Shepherd and the two PKs opened up at the same time. Paxton was just a fraction of a second slower. Shepherd let fly on full auto, spraying back and forth across the Boars' grills, hoping to disable them.

Paxton had only three-round bursts available to him, but he tried to put them to their best effect. His first two bursts went into the windshield of the nearer vehicle, covering it with a spider web of cracks. Less than half of his bullets connected, however, due to range and the motion between the target and his firing platform.

Shepherd's spray of bullets didn't do much either, as most of his shots bounced harmlessly off armor plating or punched out headlights.

The opposition's return fire was far more effective. The first burst from the two PKs tore up the ground right behind the fleeing Ural then stitched two jagged lines upward through the rear of the truck. Both of its back two tires were hit and came apart all over the road. The rear end shimmied and skidded back and forth a second before Cross could regain control.

The wooden tailgate was shredded. All three

soldiers in front of the civilians took hits on their body armor. Jannati also took a hit in the shoulder, while Williams caught one in the meat of his thigh. Howard took one in the small of his back right under the edge of his armor. Yamashita was the only one to make it through without any extra hits. Despite their efforts, one of the civilians was hit as well, and his scream rose above the chaos of battle.

Shepherd and Paxton took the worst of it. The opening barrage knocked them both back. Paxton wound up sitting down hard, clutching his M4 in one hand. He couldn't feel his legs, and his left arm lay heavy and useless at his side. His ears rang, and he was dizzy from a bullet that glanced off his helmet.

Unable to see over the tailgate, he forced his rifle up over the edge and squeezed the trigger over and over again, blind-firing at the vehicles behind. He couldn't see what happened, but one of his bursts connected with the windshield he'd already hit once, covering it with more holes and cracks. He didn't hit the driver — the windshield was evidently bullet-proof glass — but he made it so hard to see that the driver missed a curve in the road and ran into a ditch. Its gunner tried to fire again, but the Boar's erratic path made it impossible to aim straight.

When Paxton's weapon ran dry, he looked over at Shepherd. For all he could tell, Shepherd was dead. The gunfire had knocked him flat on his back with his knees up and his machine gun between them. Blood pooled on the cargo bed beneath him. Through his own haze of pain and shock, Paxton couldn't see Shepherd's chest moving.

"Mark!" Paxton barked at his fellow Green Beret. "Mark, get up!"

Somehow, from somewhere at the edge of life, Shepherd heard his name. His eyes popped open. He groaned and coughed up a mouthful of blood.

And then he got mad.

His eyes blazing, his lips pulled back from red-stained teeth in a snarl, he heaved himself back upright like a zombie lurching back to life. He couldn't lift his machine gun high enough to put it over the top of the tailgate, so he kicked out with both legs and broke the tattered, bullet-ruined panel right off the back of the truck.

# RAT-A-TAT-A-TAT-A-TAT-TAT!
## RAT-A-TAT-A-TAT-A-TAT-TAT!

Fire bloomed from his M240 as he clenched the trigger in a death grip. The weapon bucked in his hand, throwing bullets wildly out the back. One of them punched out the second boar's last remaining headlight. A few cracked the windshield. And some, miraculously, found the gunner behind the PK and threw him off the back of the vehicle. The boar swerved and slowed down, though it didn't leave the road.

Shepherd's ammo box ran out. He dropped the empty weapon beside him.

"That a boy," Paxton said. "Now come here."

Wild-eyed, Shepherd rolled over on one side toward Paxton, who dragged himself one-armed to meet him halfway. When they were side-by-side, Paxton unhooked an M67 fragmentation grenade from his web belt. He managed to get rid of the safety one-handed.

"Give me a hand with this," Paxton said.

Shepherd, barely aware of his surroundings, held out his good hand. Paxton hooked the ring of the pin over his finger.

"Pull," Paxton said.

Shepherd's finger flexed. Together, they managed to yank the pin out, though the effort made a gray cloud close in around the edges of Paxton's vision. Fortunately, he kept the spoon tight against the side of the grenade so it didn't go off.

Meanwhile, the boar that had gone off the road pulled off and disappeared into the darkness. The other one, however, picked up speed once more, and a new gunner climbed up behind the PK. Paxton saw the man aim the machine gun's barrel toward the rear of the truck. Over the road noise and the engines, Paxton could hear the man calling his name. But it couldn't have been his voice, could it? He didn't know his name. The voice had to be coming from somewhere else.

*Doesn't matter,* Paxton thought. They wouldn't be able to take another barrage of bullets. He had to do something. They only had a few seconds.

Paxton's weak, blood-slicked fingers freed the spoon. It popped off the grenade.

*Five,* he counted in his head.

*Four . . .*

Gray closed in. The machine gunner took aim. Someone said his name again.

*Three . . .*

With a hideous gasp, Shepherd collapsed once more and was still.

Paxton closed his eyes.

*Two . . .*

He threw the grenade. It bounced onto the road and disappeared in the dust.

*One . . .*

Paxton passed out.

* * *

"Paxton!" Cross shouted, fighting to keep the damaged truck on the narrow dirt road. Not only were the back tires out, but the thing was leaking fuel, and a dozen warning lights flickered on the dashboard. "Paxton, what's happening back —"

# KABOOOOOOOM!!.

A grenade explosion cut him off. The blast sounded like it had gone off in the cab with him. For a split second he thought it had come from the boar, putting an end to their Ural truck's desperate flight.

But a glance in the side mirror showed him the truth: the blast had gone off right under the boar's front driver-side tire, blowing the wheel off and taking out the engine. Black smoke streamed from the vehicle as it skidded to a halt. For the few seconds Cross could spare to watch it, no one got out of the vehicle and no more shots came from its machine gun.

"Somebody talk to me!" Cross demanded.

"We've got wounded," Yamashita said. "One civilian took a flesh wound. Williams caught one in the leg, through-and-through. Jannati's shoulder is in pieces. Howard's hit in the back. Williams is doing what he can, but they're out of the fight. Howard might not make it."

Yamashita paused, took a deep breath, then exhaled in a hiss of pain. "Paxton and Shepherd are dead."

Lancaster clenched her teeth and whispered to herself. Cross couldn't make out the words.

"I only saw one of the boars go down," Cross said, shoving all the other information away to be processed later. "Are both of the vehicles out of commission?"

"Negative," Yamashita said. "We only slowed the first one down. It's making its way back to the road now. I can see it in my Leupold. Looks like it's heading for the wreckage of the second boar. I figure they'll take on survivors and pick up the chase again."

"Anything you can do from here?" Cross asked.

"I'm sorry, Commander," Yamashita said. "They're moving, the truck's moving, and they're too far away. Maybe when they get closer . . . I don't know. How much more road do we have left?"

Cross looked at Lancaster. "How much farther?"

"We're close," Lancaster said, her face pale and drawn. She seemed to be fighting back the urge to throw up. "We're close, but . . . they're still going to get to us before we get across into Erbil."

"A lot of road," Cross told Yamashita.

"Then stop," Yamashita said. "I'm not hurt, and there's only one boar left. I can slow it down when it comes in range."

"Too risky," Cross said. "If I stop this thing long enough for you to do that, I might not be able to get it going again. And if we have to walk our wounded from here to Erbil, we'll all be sitting ducks if anyone else comes looking for us."

"I didn't say wait, Commander," Yamashita said so softly that Cross barely heard him. "Just slow down long enough for me to get out. I'll keep them off you and watch the road for anybody else. When you get past the safe point, call me. I'll reel in."

"Kim . . ."

"Sir, this isn't a hard decision. It's the only option you've got. Besides, I've been doing a lot of thinking about the talk we had before we got here. I figured out the answer to my question. The one about why you're willing to risk your life."

Cross's stomach sank. "Tell me."

"Us," Yamashita replied. "You risk your life to keep us safe, so we can get the job done. That's your answer, isn't it, Commander?"

Cross's eyes blurred. He blinked to clear them. "That's exactly the reason, Lieutenant."

"Mine, too," Yamashita said. "Now let me out of the truck."

Cross slowed and pulled over. "Do what you have to do," he said.

"Sir," Yamashita said. A moment later, he added, "Okay, I'm out. Get moving."

"Erbil's not far now, Lieutenant," Cross told him. "I'll reel you in as soon as we get there."

"Sir," Yamashita said. "Out."

"Good luck, Kim," Cross said. "And thank you. Out."

* * *

Yamashita waited for several seconds as the Ural drove away to make sure Cross wouldn't change his mind and turn around. When he was satisfied

the Commander wasn't coming back, he dug the canalphone out of his ear, dropped it on the ground, and crushed it with his heel.

"Sorry, Commander," he whispered, smiling sadly. "I'd reel in if I could, but we both know that's not an option."

He took a deep breath, wincing due to a cracked rib under his armor vest. Then he moved off to a low hillside that offered him the best firing angle over the road. The undamaged boar was idling next to its damaged counterpart, and soldiers from the latter were climbing into the former. They were about 2,000 yards out.

Yamashita unscrewed the sound and flash suppressor from the end of his M110. Once he started firing, they'd see him, they'd hear him, and they'd come for him. He wouldn't give them a choice in the matter. They'd hunt him down, and he'd make them work for it. He'd waste their time by picking off as many of them as he could. As many as it took for Cross to get the others to safety like he'd promised.

As for himself . . .

"Well, I'm gonna die with a hammer in my hand, Lord, Lord," Yamashita sang. "I'm gonna die with a hammer in my hand."

# CLASSIFIED

## MISSION DEBRIEFING

### OPERATION

#### STEEL HAMMER                    012

### PRIMARY OBJECTIVES

- Sabotage ISIS supply chain

- Rendezvous with Peshmerga forces

### SECONDARY OBJECTIVES

x Secure any munitions found

### STATUS

2/3 COMPLETE

3245.98 ● ● ●

# CROSS, RYAN

RANK: Lieutenant Commander
BRANCH: Navy Seal
PSYCH PROFILE: Team leader of Shadow Squadron. Control oriented and loyal, Cross insisted on hand-picking each member of his squad.

We incurred heavy losses on this mission. We also saved many innocent lives. Adam Paxton, Mark Shepherd, Carter Howard, and Kimiyo Yamashita died the way they lived: in selfless service of the innocent and as our brothers-in-arms.

We've lost team members before. We will lose team members again. But Shadow Squadron will persevere as an ideal, as the invisible arm of liberty, as a memorial to those who sacrificed their lives for all of us.

– Lieutenant Commander Ryan Cross

## *ERROR*

### UNAUTHORIZED

USER MUST HAVE LEVEL 12 CLEARANCE
OR HIGHER IN ORDER TO GAIN ACCESS
TO FURTHER MISSION INFORMATION.

2019.681

## CREATOR BIO(S)

AUTHOR

# CARL BOWEN

Carl Bowen is a father, husband, and writer living in Lawrenceville, Georgia. He was born in Louisiana, lived briefly in England, and was raised in Georgia where he went to school. He has published a handful of novels, short stories, and comics. For Stone Arch Books, he has retold *20,000 Leagues Under the Sea*, *The Strange Case of Dr. Jekyll and Mr. Hyde*, *The Jungle Book*, *Aladdin and the Magic Lamp*, *Julius Caesar*, and *The Murders in the Rue Morgue*. He is the original author of *BMX Breakthrough* as well as the Shadow Squadron series.

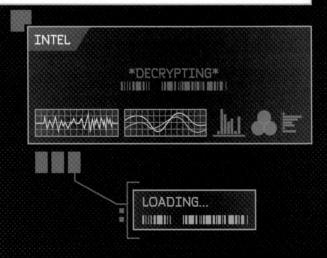

INTEL

*DECRYPTING*

LOADING...

ARTIST

# WILSON TORTOSA

Wilson "Wunan" Tortosa is a Filipino comic book artist best known for his work on *Tomb Raider* and the American relaunch of *Battle of the Planets* for Top Cow Productions. Wilson attended Philippine Cultural High School, then went on to the University of Santo Tomas where he graduated with a Bachelor's Degree in Fine Arts, majoring in Advertising.

ARTIST

# BENNY FUENTES

Benny Fuentes lives in Villahermosa, Tabasco, in Mexico, where the temperature is just as hot as the sauce. He studied graphic design in college, but now he works as a full-time illustrator in the comic book and graphic novel industry for companies like Marvel, DC Comics, and Top Cow Productions. He shares his home with two crazy cats, Chelo and Kitty, who act like they own the place.

2019.681

# CLASSIFIED

## AUTHOR DEBRIEFING

**ACCESS GRANTED**

### CARL BOWEN

Q/When and why did you decide to become a writer?
A/I've enjoyed writing ever since I was in elementary school. I wrote as much as I could, hoping to become the next Lloyd Alexander or Stephen King, but I didn't sell my first story until I was in college. It had been a long wait, but the day I saw my story in print was one of the best days of my life.

Q/What made you decide to write *Shadow Squadron*?
A/As a kid, my heroes were always brave knights or noble loners who fought because it was their duty, not for fame or glory. I think the special ops soldiers of the US military embody those ideals. Their jobs are difficult and often thankless, so I wanted to show how cool their jobs are and also express my gratitude for our brave warriors.

Q/What inspires you to write?
A/My biggest inspiration is my family. My wife's love and support lifts me up when this job seems too hard to keep going. My son is another big inspiration.

He's three years old, and I want him to read my books and feel the same way I did when I read my favorite books as a kid. And if he happens to grow up to become an elite soldier in the US military, that would be pretty awesome, too.

Q/Describe what it was like to write these books.
A/The only military experience I have is a year I spent in the Army ROTC. It gave me a great respect for the military and its soldiers, but I quickly realized I would have made a pretty awful soldier. I recently got to test out a friend's arsenal of firearms, including a combat shotgun, an AR-15 rifle, and a Barrett M82 sniper rifle. We got to blow apart an old fax machine.

Q/What is your favorite book, movie, and game?
A/My favorite book of all time is *Don Quixote*. It's crazy and it makes me laugh. My favorite movie is either *Casablanca* or *Double Indemnity*, old black-and-white movies made before I was born. My favorite game, hands down, is *Skyrim*, in which you play a heroic dragonslayer. But not even *Skyrim* can keep me from writing more *Shadow Squadron* stories, so you won't have to wait long to read more about Ryan Cross and his team. That's a promise.

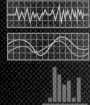

## COM CHATTER

-MISSION PREVIEW: After an unknown aircraft crashes in Antarctica near a science facility, Shadow Squadron is deployed to recover the device. But when Russian special forces intervene, Cross gets caught between the mission's objective and the civilian scientists' safety.

3245.98 ● ● ●

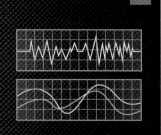

PHANTOM SUN

CARL BOWEN

# PHANTOM SUN

Cross tapped his touchscreen to start the video. On the screen, a few geologists began pointing and waving frantically. The camera watched them all for another couple of seconds then lurched around in a half circle and tilted skyward. Blurry clouds wavered in and out of focus for a second before the cameraman found what the others had pointing at — a lance of white fire in the sky. The image focused, showing what appeared to be a meteorite with a trailing white plume behind it punching through a hole in the clouds. The camera zoomed out to allow the cameraman to better track the object's progress through the sky.

"Is that a meteorite?" Shepherd asked.

"Just keep watching," Brighton said, breathless with anticipation.

Right on cue, the supposed meteorite suddenly flared white, then changed directions in mid-flight by almost 45 degrees. Grunts and hisses of surprise filled the room.

"So . . . not a meteorite," Shepherd muttered.

The members of Shadow Squadron watched in awe as the falling object changed direction once again with another flare and then pitched downward. The camera angle twisted overhead and then lowered to track its earthward trajectory from below.

"And now . . . sonic boom," Brighton said.

The camera image shook violently for a second as the compression wave from the falling object broke the speed of sound and as the accompanying burst shook the cameraman's hands. A moment later, the object streaked into the distance and disappeared into the rolling hills of ice and snow. The video footage ended a few moments later with a still image of the

gawking geologists looking as excited as a bunch of kids on Christmas morning.

"This video popped up on the Internet a few hours ago," Cross began. "It's already starting to go viral."

"What is it?" Second Lieutenant Aram Jannati said. Jannati, the team's newest member, came from the Marine Special Operations Regiment. "I can't imagine we'd get involved if it was just a meteor."

"Meteorite," Staff Sergeant Adam Paxton corrected. "If it gets through the atmosphere to the ground, it's a meteorite."

"That wasn't a meteorite, man," Brighton said, hopping out of his chair. He dug his smartphone out of a cargo pocket and came around the table toward the front of the room. He laid his phone on the touchscreen Cross had used and then synced up the two devices. With that done, he used his phone as a remote control to run the video backward to the first time the object had changed directions. He used a slider to move the timer back and forth, showing the object's fairly sharp angle of deflection through the sky.

"Meteorites can't change directions like this," Brighton said. "This is 45 degrees of deflection at least, and the thing barely even slows down."

"I'm seeing a flare when it turns," Paxton said. "Meteors hold a lot of frozen water when they're in space, and it expands when it reaches the atmosphere. If those gases are venting or exploding, couldn't that cause a change of direction?"

"Not this sharply," Brighton said before Cross could reply. "Besides, if you look at this…" He used a few swipes across his phone to pause the video and zoom in on the flying object. At the new resolution, a dark, oblong shape was visible inside a wreath of fire. He then advanced through the first and second changes of direction and tracked it a few seconds forward before pausing again. "See?"

A room full of shrugs and uncomprehending looks met Brighton's eager gaze.

"It's the same size!" Brighton said, tossing his hands up in mock frustration. "If this thing had exploded twice — with enough force to push something this big in a different direction both times — it would be in a million pieces. So those aren't explosions. They're thrusters or ramjets or something."

"Which makes this what?" Shepherd asked. "A UFO?"

"Sure," Paxton answered in a mocking tone. "It's unidentified, it's flying, and it's surely an object. It probably has little green men inside, too."

"You don't know that it doesn't," Brighton said. "I mean, this thing could be from outer space!"

"Sit down, Sergeant," Chief Walker said.

Brighton reluctantly did so, pocketing his phone.

"Don't get ahead of yourself, Ed," Cross said, retaking control of the briefing. "Phantom Cell analysts have authenticated the video and concluded that this thing isn't just a meteorite. It's some kind of metal construct, though they can't make out specifics from the quality of the video. I suppose it's possible it's from outer space, but it's much more likely it's man-made. All we know for sure is that it's not American made. Therefore, our mission is to get out to where it came down, secure it, zip it up, and bring it back for a full analysis. Anyone have any questions so far?"

"I do," Jannati said. "What is Phantom Cell?"

Cross nodded. Jannati was the newest member of the team, and as such he wasn't as familiar with all the various secret programs. "Phantom Cell is a parallel program to ours," Cross explained. "But their focus is on psy-ops, cyberwarfare, and research and development."

Jannati nodded. "Geeks, in other words," he said.

Brighton gave him a sour look but said nothing.

"What are we supposed to do about the scientists who found this thing?" Lieutenant Kimiyo Yamashita asked. True to his stoic nature, the sniper had finished his breakfast and coffee while everyone else was talking excitedly. "Do they know we're coming?"

"That's the problem," Cross said, frowning. "We haven't heard a peep out of them since this video appeared online. Attempts at contacting them have gone unanswered. Last anyone heard, the geologists who made the video were going to try to find the point of impact where this object came down. We have no idea whether they found it or not, or what happened to them."

"Isn't this how the movie *Aliens* started?" Brighton asked. "With a space colony suddenly cutting off communication after a UFO crash landing?"

Paxton rolled his eyes. "Lost Aspen, the base there, is pretty new," he said. "And it's in the middle of Antarctica. It could just be a simple technical failure."

"You have zero imagination, man," Brighton said. "You're going to be the first one the monster eats. Well... after me, anyway."

"These are our orders," Cross continued as if he had never been interrupted. "Find what crashed, bring the object back for study, figure out why the research station stopped communicating, and make sure the civilians are safe. Stealth is going to be of paramount importance on this one. Nobody has any territorial claims on Marie Byrd Land, but no country is supposed to be sending troops on missions anywhere in Antarctica, either."

"Are we expecting anyone else to be breaking that rule while we are, Commander?" Yamashita asked.

"It's possible," Cross said. "If this object is man-made, whoever made it is probably going to come looking for it. Any other government that attached the same significance to the video that ours did could send people, too. No specific intel has been confirmed yet, but it's only a matter of time before someone takes an active interest."

"Seems like the longer the video's out there, the more likely we're going to have company," Yamashita said.

"About that," Cross said with a mischievous smile on his face. "Phantom Cell's running a psy-ops campaign in support of our efforts. They're simultaneously spreading the word that the video's a hoax and doing their best to stop it from spreading and to remove it from circulation."

"Good luck to them on that last one," Brighton snorted. "It's the Internet. Phantom Cell's good, but nobody's that good."

"Not our concern," Cross said. "We ship out in one hour. Get your gear on the Commando. We'll go over more mission specifics during the flight. Understood?"

"Sir," the men responded in unison. At a nod from Cross, they rose and gathered up the remains of their breakfast. As they left the briefing room, Walker remained behind. He gulped down the last of his coffee before standing up.

"Brighton's sure excited," Walker said.

"I knew he would be," Cross replied. "I didn't expect him to try to help out so much with the briefing, though."

"Is that what I'm like whenever I chip in from up here?" Walker asked.

Cross fought off the immediate urge to toy with his second-in-command, though he couldn't stop the mischievous smile from coming back. "Maybe a little bit," he said.

Walker returned Cross's grin. "Then I wholeheartedly apologize."

*TRANSMISSION ERROR*

PLEASE CONTACT YOUR LOCAL LIBRARY OR BOOKSTORE FOR MORE DETAILS...

2012.101